That's What a Friend Is

P. K. Hallinan

This book is a gift of love

To ———————————————————

From ———————————————————

ideals children's books
Nashville, Tennessee

ISBN 0-8249-5390-8 (case)

ISBN 0-8249-5391-6 (paper)

Published by Ideals Children's Books

An imprint of Ideals Publications

A division of Guideposts

535 Metroplex Drive, Suite 250

Nashville, Tennessee 37211

www.idealspublications.com

Printed and bound in Mexico by RR Donnelley & Sons.

Library of Congress CIP data on file.

Books by P. K. Hallinan

A Rainbow of Friends

For the Love of Our Earth

Heartprints

How Do I Love You?

I'm Thankful Each Day!

Just Open a Book

Let's Learn All We Can!

My Dentist, My Friend

My Doctor, My Friend

My First Day of School

My Teacher's My Friend

That's What a Friend Is

Today Is Christmas!

Today Is Easter!

Today Is Halloween!

Today Is Thanksgiving!

Today Is Valentine's Day!

Today Is Your Birthday!

We're Very Good Friends, My Brother and I

We're Very Good Friends, My Father and I

We're Very Good Friends, My Grandma and I

We're Very Good Friends, My Grandpa and I

We're Very Good Friends, My Mother and I

We're Very Good Friends, My Sister and I

When I Grow Up

10 9 8 7 6 5 4

A friend is a listener
who'll always
be there

when you've got a big
secret
you just have to share.

A friend is a sidekick
who'll sit by your side

to make you feel better
when you're troubled inside.

And when there's nothing to do
on a wet rainy day,

a friend is a pal
who'll come over to play.

Friends are just perfect
for all kinds of things,

like walking...
or talking ...

or swinging on swings!

And for watching TV,
a friend is the best

for cheering cartoons
and booing the rest.
with,

And then late at night
a friend is just right

for telling ghost stories
when you've turned off
the light.

Yes, a friend is the best one
to hop, skip, or run with...

You can sing and shout
'til your tonsils wear out,

'cause that's what having
a friend's all about!

A friend is a buddy
who'll come to your aid

when he thinks you need
help,
or you might be afraid.

A friend is a partner who'll stand back to back to protect you from bullies, or a monster attack.

With a friend you can do
what you most like to do!

You can have your own
hideouts

in dark, secret places...

or spend the whole day having caterpillar races.

or just drawing pictures
of each other's faces.

You can laugh...

you can cry...

you can watch cars
go by...

you can have a great time
and not even try!

A friend is a person
who likes to be there...

'cause you two
make a wonderful pair!

And when all's said and done,
the natural end is ...

a friend is a friend... THAT'S what a friend is!